THE OFFICIAL
QUEENS PARK RANGERS
ANNUAL 2015

Written by Francis Atkinson & Ian Taylor

Designed by Lucy Boyd

A Grange Publication

© 2014. Published by Grange Communications Ltd., Edinburgh, under licence from the Queens Park Rangers Football Club. Printed in the EU.

Photographs © Back Page Images.

ISBN: 978-1-908925-71-8

£7.99

CONTENTS

P6   2013/2014 Season Review

P12   Wembley Awaits

P14   We Did It – The Wembley Way

P18   Robert Green Poster

P19   Spot the Ball

P20   Player Profiles

P29   Harry Redknapp Poster

P30   Charlie Wins Awards Quadruple!

P32   Fan-tastic Support!

P34   Dressed to Impress in the Premier League

P36   QPR Quiz

P38   Pre-Season Diary

P44   Joey Barton Poster

P45   Charlie Austin Poster

P46   Nedum Onuoha Poster

P47   Wordsearch

P50   Charlie, Charlie, Charlie, Austin…

P52   Junior Hoilett Poster

P53   Matt Phillips Poster

P54   Rio Ferdinand Interview – Exclusive

P56   Interesting Facts

P58   Jordon Mutch Poster

P59   Yun Suk-young Poster

P60   Quiz Answers

P62   Where's Spark?

2013/14 SEASON REVIEW

AS EXPECTED, IT WAS A REAL ROLLERCOASTER OF A SEASON FOR QPR – A CAMPAIGN THAT PROMISED SO MUCH AND THEN ULTIMATELY DELIVERED ON THE BIGGEST STAGE OF THEM ALL IN THE CHAMPIONSHIP PLAY-OFF FINAL AT WEMBLEY. BUT HOW DID WE GET THERE?

AUGUST – SUPER START

Despite our second round League Cup exit at the hands of Swindon Town, Rangers started the season in fine fashion. We kicked off the campaign with a 2-1 home victory over Sheffield Wednesday – thanks to goals from Nedum Onuoha and Andy Johnson – before Capital One Cup success three days later in the first round at Exeter City. New signings Charlie Austin and Danny Simpson scored their first goals for the

Hoops in Devon. A Championship draw away at Huddersfield Town followed, Junior Hoilett on the scoresheet, before the R's won four league games on the spin – three in August, the other in September. Ipswich Town, Bolton Wanderers and Leeds United (all 1-0) were rumbled in the opening month, youngster Tom Hitchcock, Johnson and captain Clint Hill respectively with the goals.

SEPTEMBER – TOP OF THE SHOP

QPR raced to the top of the Championship table after our good start to the season continued. The month began in positive fashion with victory over Birmingham City in W12, Austin on target for the first time in the league for Rangers. That result was followed by a close home draw, 0-0, against Brighton & Hove Albion, before two more September wins followed. Austin's penalty was the difference in a dogged display against Championship newcomers Yeovil Town, before Middlesbrough were dispatched 2-0 in front of the Loftus Road faithful, with goals from the restored Joey Barton and Austin. September also saw August arrival Matty Phillips come into the side after an arm injury.

OCTOBER – MIXED MONTH

The month of October was a mixed one, with the R's eventually dropping to third in the league table. Things started well with a 2-1 home success over Barnsley, as Rangers set a new club record after an eighth consecutive clean sheet and Austin with both goals in a comfortable win, but the Hoops twice surrendered the lead at Millwall – after goals from Niko Kranjcar and Austin –to draw 2-2, the Lions' second arriving deep into added time after the break. Then came QPR's first defeat of the campaign, a 2-0 reverse in a promotion tussle at Burnley. October ended with a goalless draw at the DW Stadium – home to Wigan Athletic.

NOVEMBER – FAURLIN INJURED ON RETURN OF THE MAC

A four-game month saw Rangers go three unbeaten before defeat at the end of November. Harry Redknapp's men returned to winning ways with a 2-1 scoreline against Derby County, Jermaine Jenas and John Eustace (own goal) on target as former coach Steve McClaren revisited Loftus Road as Rams manager. The result, however, was marred following a serious injury to Ale Faurlin – ending his season. Barton showed support for his Argentine team-mate by holding Faurlin's shirt aloft after netting in a 1-1 draw at Reading, and Rangers registered another victory thanks to Austin's goal-of-the-season contender in a 1-0 win over Charlton Athletic on home soil. The month came to a close following a 2-1 loss at Doncaster Rovers, Rangers leaving Yorkshire with nothing to show despite Austin giving the Hoops a 43rd-minute lead.

DECEMBER – HARD WORK UNDONE

The R's produced one of their best displays of the season – a 3-0 success over Bournemouth – to kick off the festive month in style and, after a dominant 2-0 win at Blackpool followed a home stalemate with Blackburn Rovers, Austin and Phillips scoring the goals, QPR returned to the summit of the division. However, Christmas wasn't so kind to Redknapp's side. First, Jamie Vardy's effort secured victory for eventual champions Leicester City in front of the live Sky Sports cameras at Loftus Road, before Rangers fell to a comprehensive 2-0 defeat at Nottingham Forest on Boxing Day. A trip to Vicarage Road at the end of December saw Watford and QPR play out an uneventful 0-0 draw.

JANUARY – RANGERS RESURGENT BUT AUSTIN BLOW

January was much better for Rangers – four wins coming from as many league games, in fact, aside from defeat in the FA Cup third round at Everton – but QPR were dealt a bitter blow come the end of the month. An injury to top scorer Austin meant the striker was to miss the majority of the remainder of the campaign, and the Hoops struggled to replace his goals to sustain their automatic-promotion push thereafter. Austin, along with Phillips, was on target in a 2-1 home victory over Doncaster Rovers on New Year's Day, while a superb 3-1 win at Ipswich followed defeat in the FA Cup– Kranjcar, Gary O'Neil and Armand Traore all scoring. Austin's injury came following a 2-1 success against Bolton in west London, the striker himself and Karl Henry netting the goals. Meanwhile, Redknapp added a number of new names to his squad ahead of the transfer deadline. Kevin Doyle, Will Keane, Modibo Maiga and Ravel Morrison were all acquired on loan, while Aaron Hughes joined permanently from near-neighbours Fulham.

FEBRUARY – HOPES HURT

After winning their place back in the top two following an excellent January, the R's would slip out of the automatic-promotion places and never return following a February to forget. It all started with a thrilling 3-3 home draw against Burnley, Doyle and Maiga – alongside Richard Dunne – scoring on their debuts in front of a live Sky audience. But three defeats put a serious dent in QPR's challenge. First former coach McClaren came back to haunt Rangers when his Derby team took a 1-0 victory at the iPro Stadium. And then came two more defeats as Reading claimed a 3-1 victory at Loftus Road, Doyle on the scoresheet against his former team, and the Hoops fell to a last-minute loss at Charlton. The misery was compounded with the news that winger Phillips would miss the rest of the campaign through injury.

MARCH – LOANEE LIFTS R'S

With eight games, it was a busy month, but a largely profitable one, with four wins and two draws. Morrison, following his loan move from West Ham United, lit up March with five goals. The month started with a 1-1 home draw with Leeds, Jenas scoring, before a Morrison brace in our 2-0 victory at Birmingham. A 3-0 home rout of Yeovil – goals coming from Morrison (two) and Bobby Zamora – was sandwiched in between defeats at both Brighton and Sheffield Wednesday, but Rangers went unbeaten thereafter. Yossi Benayoun, Zamora and Morrison all found the net in a 3-1 win at Middlesbrough, before the R's saw off Wigan 1-0 in W12 just three days later, Benayoun on target once again. The Hoops then shared the spoils with Blackpool at Loftus Road after a late Hoilett effort.

APRIL – PLAY-OFFS SECURED

April ended with three defeats in six Championship outings for Rangers – though Redknapp's men did secure their place in the end-of-season Play-Offs, as well as fourth place in the table. It was an unwelcome start to the month, with defeats coming at both Bournemouth (2-1) and Blackburn (2-0) – Traore scoring our goal on the South Coast. But QPR fans were treated to a goal-fest at Loftus Road on April 12th, as the R's overcame Nottingham Forest 5-2. There were also five different goal scorers, as Benayoun, Hoilett, Onuoha, Morrison and Zamora all got in on the act. Defeat at champions Leicester followed, before another exciting home contest, Rangers coming from behind to beat Watford 2-1 thanks to goals from Barton and Austin – the latter finding the net in second-half injury time. There was another stoppage-time strike in W12 later that week, but this time for visitors Millwall, who recovered to score at the death after an Austin penalty had put the Hoops in the driving seat.

MAY – PLAY-OFFS LOOM LARGE

Rangers rounded off the season with a 3-2 win at Barnsley, memorable for Charlie Austin's 100th goal in the professional game. Yun Suk Young's first goal in Rangers colours was an absolute cracker too, as Harry Redknapp's side headed into the Play-Offs brimming with confidence.

WEMBLEY AWAITS

RANGERS FACED WIGAN ATHLETIC IN THE CHAMPIONSHIP PLAY-OFF SEMI-FINALS, WITH THE FIRST LEG AT THE DW STADIUM ON FRIDAY 9TH MAY.

The Latics headed into the two-legged tie as firm favourites, with their 'big game' experience – just a year on from them lifting the FA Cup – referred to throughout by experts in the build up to the clash in Lancashire.

In front of 3,000-plus travelling R's supporters, however, it was Harry Redknapp's men who headed back to London with the slightest of advantages.

Chances were at a premium throughout the first leg tie, with goalkeepers Rob Green and Scott Carson spectators for much of the clash. After Armand Traore headed over midway through the half, Green was perfectly positioned to keep out Jordi Gomez's stinging drive.

Marc Antoine Fortune spurned the best chance of note when he lashed over from close range late on, as the game ended goalless, setting up a nervy second leg in W12 three days later.

The nerves were cranked up a notch amongst the home faithful when James Perch slotted Wigan in front in the opening nine minutes at Loftus Road.

Perch fired home from close range, to hand Uwe Rosler's men the perfect start at a packed Loftus Road. Undeterred – and with the Hoops faithful in full voice – Charlie Austin restored parity with a 73rd minute leveller from the spot to send the clash into extra-time.

And then came THE moment in the sixth minute of extra-time. Substitute Bobby Zamora crossed from the right and Austin powered past his marker to touch home and send the Hoops faithful into ecstasy. Rangers were on their way to Wembley …

WE DID IT –
THE WEMBLEY WAY

'ZAMORA! UNBELIEVABLE … FROM THE VERY BRINK OF ELIMINATION, BOBBY ZAMORA HAS SURELY SCORED ANOTHER PLAY-OFF WINNER.' THE WORDS OF SKY SPORTS COMMENTATOR BILL LESLIE FOLLOWING THE GOAL THAT BOOKED OUR RETURN TO THE BARCLAYS PREMIER LEAGUE – ETCHED ON THE MINDS OF ALL WHO, IF THEY'RE ANYTHING LIKE MYSELF, CONTINUE TO REPLAY THAT MOMENT OVER AND AGAIN. MANY HAVE CALLED OUR CHAMPIONSHIP PLAY-OFF FINAL WIN OVER DERBY COUNTY THEIR 'GREATEST EVER QPR MOMENT'. WHATEVER IT IS FOR YOU – HERE'S A RECAP …

DERBY COUNTY 0, QPR 1
Championship Play-Off Final
Saturday 24th May 2014

Ten-man QPR pulled off the unlikeliest of victories to win promotion back to the Premier League at the first attempt after a 1-0 Championship Play-Off final win over Derby County at Wembley.

It was unlikely because Harry Redknapp's men had Gary

O'Neil sent off for a straight red card in the 60th minute, following a late, last-ditch challenge on Johnny Russell.

But Rangers rode the Rams storm and, when Junior Hoilett crossed for substitute Bobby Zamora in the final minute of normal time, he finished emphatically to hand the R's a place back in the top division.

Redknapp named an unchanged side following our semi-final, second leg victory over Wigan Athletic at Loftus Road.

Rob Green started in goal, behind a back four of Danny Simpson, Richard Dunne, Nedum Onuoha and Clint Hill.

Hoilett, Joey Barton, O'Neil and Niko Kranjcar began in midfield.

Top scorer Charlie Austin was paired with Kevin Doyle in attack.

Half of Wembley was a sea of blue and white thanks to specially-made flags given to every QPR supporter.

And there was incredible noise, too, as the players came out for kick-off.

Unsurprisingly, the opening stanza made for a close-run contest. Both teams were eager to stamp their mark on this final from the outset.

Rangers had the first shot in anger. Austin controlled a Barton header on eight minutes before firing over from 25 yards.

However, chances were few and far between inside the first quarter hour.

QPR players were already putting their bodies on the line. A succession of strong tackles in the 17th minute got R's fans on their feet.

Derby enjoyed their first opportunity in the 25th minute. Jamie Ward's deep centre from the left was met at the back post by Craig Forsyth, but he could only head wide – albeit from an acute angle.

The Rams had claims for a penalty turned down three minutes later when Will Hughes clashed with Dunne. Referee Lee Mason waved away the appeals.

Hughes also shot over from 20 yards out in the 32nd minute.

Unfortunately, the R's were forced into an early change – Kranjcar's afternoon coming to a premature end with what appeared to be a hamstring injury. Armand Traore came on in his place.

Russell saw a deflected shot caught by Green on 36 minutes. Five minutes later, the QPR goalkeeper was again called into action – tipping a low Hughes free-kick around his left-hand post.

At the other end, Rangers broke on the counter attack a minute before half-time – substitute Traore subsequently dragged wide after a Hill pass.

The sides went in all-square at the break.

In a similar vein to the first half, the start to the second period was tight.

Derby had a succession of corner kicks inside the opening 10 minutes, but that was about as good as it got. Both sets of fans tried to rally their respective teams.

The best chance of the contest yet came in the 57th minute. Traore crossed for Austin – and he dragged his shot just wide.

Doyle made way for Zamora straight after that incident. Austin blazed over from Hoilett in the 58th minute.

QPR's claims were dealt a bitter blow on the hour when O'Neil was dismissed.

Russell was played though on goal and when he took the ball in his stride, O'Neil came in with a challenge from behind to foul the attacker.

Referee Mason consulted with his linesman before brandishing a straight red card.

Redknapp responded by bringing on Karl Henry for skipper Hill in the 67th minute.

Two minutes later, Green pulled off a smart, low stop to save from sub Craig Bryson. The QPR custodian then produced a stunning reaction block to thwart Chris Martin.

A man down, Rangers had to put in the hard yards to stay in the final – and Green had to be at his best.

The Hoops number one was just that when fashioning a fine stop to deny Simon Dawkins at point-blank range.

The final 10 minutes were nervy as the R's tried to hang on, riding wave after wave of attack. Green saved from Bryson with two minutes left to play.

Rangers soon had a now-rare attack, from which Barton blasted wide.

Against all the odds, QPR stole victory with a goal in the 90th minute.

Hoilett did fantastically well to win possession on the right-hand by-line and when his cross wasn't dealt with, Zamora diverted home to send R's fans wild.

What a season – and, in typical Rangers style, what an end to it!

Derby County (4-2-3-1): Grant; Wisdom, Keogh, Buxton, Forsyth; Thorne, Hughes (Bryson 68); Hendrick, Russell (Dawkins 67), Ward (Bamford 90); Martin.

Subs not used: Legzdins, Whitbread, Eustace, Sammon.

Queens Park Rangers (4-4-2): Green; Simpson, Onuoha, Dunne, Hill (Henry 67); Hoilett, Barton, O'Neil, Kranjcar (Traore 33); Austin, Doyle (Zamora 57).

Subs not used: Murphy, Morrison, Suk-Young, Hughes.

Sky Bet Play-Off Final Winners 2014

Sky Bet Championship Play-Off Winners 2014

SPOT THE BALL

CAN YOU SPOT WHERE THE REAL BALL IS IN BOTH OF THE PICTURES BELOW?

ANSWERS ON PAGE 60

PLAYER PROFILES

GOALKEEPERS

ROBERT GREEN

ROB Green produced a man-of-the-match performance in QPR's moment of real need, as he helped the club win our Play-Off Final against Derby County in May 2014, despite being reduced to ten men. The former Norwich City and West Ham United goalkeeper pulled off a number of fine saves to keep the Rams out, to cap off what had been a record-breaking season for him at Loftus Road. In October 2013, Green set a club record with eight consecutive clean sheets and his role in our promotion-winning campaign cannot be underestimated. The experienced goalkeeper – who started his career as a trainee at Carrow Road – joined the R's in the summer of 2012 following the expiration of his contract at West Ham. Prior to the start of the 2014/15 campaign, he had made 67 appearances for the R's in all competitions. An international with England, Green won his first senior cap for the Three Lions in 2005 and also featured at the 2010 World Cup in South Africa. In July 2014 he signed a one-year extension, keeping him in W12 until the summer of 2015.

BRIAN MURPHY

IRISH goalkeeper Brian Murphy signed a new contract at QPR in June 2013, keeping him in W12 until the summer of 2015. Free agent Murphy joined Rangers in August 2011 but has largely been back up during his time at Loftus Road. He made his league debut for the club as a second-half substitute for the injured Rob Green against Yeovil in March 2014, and made his full debut three days later at Sheffield Wednesday. The shot-stopper began his career at Manchester City, spending time on loan at both Oldham Athletic and Peterborough United before joining Swansea City. He would later move to Bohemians and Ipswich Town. Murphy has represented the Republic of Ireland at Under-19, 20 and 21 level.

JULIO CESAR

QPR completed the capture of highly-rated Brazilian international goalkeeper Julio Cesar from Inter Milan in August 2012. Cesar made 26 appearances for the R's but was unable to prevent the club's relegation from the top flight, and spent the second half of the 2013/14 campaign on loan at Toronto FC. Current number one for his country, Cesar began his career in 1997 back in Brazil with Flamengo. He made his international bow in 2004. In January 2005, Cesar joined Italian outfit Chievo Verona before moving to Serie A giants Inter Milan, where he won an impressive five successive league titles, as well as the Champions League in 2010.

DEFENDERS

RICHARD DUNNE

REPUBLIC of Ireland international Richard Dunne brought to an end a four-year stay at Aston Villa after leaving for Loftus Road in the summer of 2013. And he was another key reason for QPR's immediate return to the Premier League, his experience helping the team form a mean defence, particularly in the opening period of the 2013/14 season. A former Everton trainee, Dunne became the Toffees youngest-ever FA Cup player when he appeared against Swindon Town in 1997. After 72 appearances and four years on Merseyside, Dunne moved to Manchester City in October 2000 and the centre-half went on to receive the club's player of the year award for four consecutive seasons. Following over 300 appearances, Dunne joined Villa – making over 100 appearances – prior to signing for QPR.

CLINT HILL

CLINT Hill joined Rangers from Crystal Palace in the summer of 2010 and was a key part of our promotion-winning side of 2010/11. His determination, passion and desire have made him a huge favourite with the QPR fans, which was best demonstrated by the fact he won the Supporters' Player of the Year award two years running while we were in the Premier League, before relegation in 2013. The centre-back, who can also operate at left back, skippered Rangers to promotion glory in 2013/14, and his selfless acts of substituting himself in our Play-Off semi-final and final for the benefit of the team only enhanced his reputation with the QPR fans. The Liverpudlian began his career with Tranmere Rovers and went on to enjoy spells at Oldham Athletic and Stoke City.

YUN SUK-YOUNG

YUN Suk-Young began his career with South Korean side Chunnam Dragons – who he left to join QPR in Janaury 2013 – after coming through the club's youth system. The highly-rated left-back made his debut for the K-League outfit just after his 19th birthday in March 2009 and would go on to feature regularly. Suk-Young broke into the R's first-team in the latter stages of our 2013/14 promotion-winning campaign, and has impressed the R's fans with his high-enery performances, and desire to get forward. He scored a stunning solo goal on the final day of the regular season in a 3-2 win at Barnsley, and played a crucial role in our Play-Off semi-final win over Wigan. Internationally, Suk-Young represented South Korea at Under-17, 20 and 23 level before making his senior debut in October 2012 against Iran in a World Cup qualifier. The Suwon-born defender played every minute of every game for South Korea in the 2014 World Cup Finals in Brazil.

PLAYER PROFILES

DEFENDERS

NEDUM ONUOHA

THE versatile Nedum Onuoha – who can play anywhere in defence – joined QPR from boyhood team Manchester City in January 2012, signing a four-and-a-half year contract. Onuoha, who is probably most comfortable at centre-back, spent 15 years with the Blues after coming up through the ranks before leaving to be reunited with former City boss Mark Hughes at Loftus Road. The defender made his England Under-21 debut in October 2005 and went on to figure in both the 2007 and 2009 European Under-21 Championship campaigns. Onuoha was a fundamental part of our strong defence in 2013/14 which helped the club make an immediate return to the Premier League.

MIDFIELDERS

JOEY BARTON

THE tough-tackling Joey Barton joined the R's from Newcastle United on a four-year deal in August 2011. A former Manchester City trainee – who he would later go on to play for at senior level – Barton enjoyed an eventful first campaign in front of his new fans after moving to QPR. He took time to win over the Loftus Road crowd but was instrumental in five consecutive home victories at the end of the 2011/12 season to help stave off relegation from the Premier League. Barton was, however, dismissed for an off-the-ball altercation in our final fixture of the campaign at Man City. The midfielder – subsequently given a lengthy ban – was loaned out to Marseille in 2012/13. He made an incredible return to QPR following the club's relegation and his leadership, desire and ability were crucial to our promotion success in 2013/14. He made 39 appearances in all competitions for the R's last term.

MIDFIELDERS

ARMAND TRAORE

SPEEDY left-midfielder Armand Traore joined the R's from Arsenal in August 2011 in search of first team football, originally as a full-back. He played a crucial role in our incredible final-day survival at Manchester City in 2011/12, setting up Jamie Mackie to give 10-man QPR a 2-1 lead with a fantastic run and cross from the left flank. QPR would survive, of course, despite an eventual 3-2 defeat. In 2013/14, Harry Redknapp converted Traore to a more attacking role in order to utilise his pace and fantastic crossing ability. In our Play-Off Final victory against Derby County, Traore come on as a first-half substitute for the injured Niko Kranjcar and, following Gary O'Neil's red card, played at left-back for the final half an hour as QPR recorded a memorable triumph. Traore enjoyed loan spells at both Portsmouth and Italian side Juventus during his time at the Emirates Stadium. A French youth and Under-21 international, he has since opted to play for Senegal at senior level.

KARL HENRY

KARL Henry joined QPR in the summer of 2013 as Harry Redknapp built a squad of players he felt could challenge for promotion. The tough-tackling midfielder made 29 outings in all competitions for the R's, including a substitute appearance in our Play-Off final victory over Derby County. Henry began his career with Stoke City where he went on to make 135 appearances between 1999 and 2006. He joined Wolves that summer in for £100,000 and went on to enjoy seven seasons at Molineux. Henry was made captain soon after and eventually led them to promotion to the Premier League in 2009. After two successful seasons fighting against relegation, Wolves dropped out of the top flight in 2012. Henry remained with the club but could do nothing to prevent the Midlanders slipping into League One before linking up with the R's.

MATT PHILLIPS

WINGER Matt Phillips joined QPR in the summer of 2013 from Blackpool, and certainly played his part in our promotion-winning season, making 21 league appearances and scoring three goals. Had it not been for injury – he missed the opening part of the campaign with a broken arm before an ankle injury ended his season in February – he would have had an even greater impact. An exciting, young talent, it will be interesting to see how he fares in the Premier League in 2014/15. Phillips started his career at Wycombe Wanderers, making his first team debut at the tender age of 17. In 2009 he was voted Wycombe's Young Player of the Year, as well as scooping the prestigious Football League Two 'Apprentice of the Year' award. That form inspired Blackpool – then a Premier League club – to sign the Aylesbury-born ace in August 2010. Despite featuring regularly for England at all youth levels, Phillips decided to commit his future to Scotland, due to his eligibility through his Scottish grandparents. He made his Scotland debut in a 5-1 friendly loss to the USA in May 2012 in Florida. He made a total of 102 appearances for Blackpool, scoring 17 goals, before his switch to Loftus Road.

MIDFIELDERS

ALEJANDRO FAURLIN

ALE Faurlin is a real fans' favourite at Loftus Road, not least for the fact he is one of the club's longest-serving players, having joined QPR prior to the 2009/10 season. The classy, creative midfielder played a starring role in our Championship-winning side of 2010/11 and the following year he started to really underline his quality with impressive performances in the Premier League. However, an ACL injury during an FA Cup encounter at MK Dons in January 2012 brought his campaign to a premature end. Faurlin returned for the 2012/13 season and made 15 appearances for the R's before joining Italian side Palermo on loan in January 2013. Following QPR's relegation from the top flight, Faurlin returned and was becoming a key figure in Harry Redknapp's promotion-chasing side before knee injury struck again, with the Argentinian's season ending in November 2013 against Derby County. Now back to full fitness for the 2014/15 season, QPR fans – and Faurlin himself, no doubt – will be hoping the player can steer clear of injuries and once again showcase his talent in the Premier League. Faurlin joined Rangers from Instituto de Cordoba in his homeland. He started his career with Rosario Central and also played for River Plate and Atletico Rafaela.

JUNIOR HOILETT

QPR signed Blackburn Rovers ace Junior Hoilett in the summer of 2012 on a four year-deal. Hoilett was out of contract at Ewood Park and, because he was under 23, a fee for his services would later be set at a tribunal. The tricky Canadian-born winger is a product of Blackburn's academy and was on their books from the age of 13. Hoilett spent time on loan at German sides Paderborn and St Pauli between 2007 and 2009 and scored against Rangers in an FA Cup tie in January 2011. Following QPR's relegation in 2013, many expected Hoilett to move on but he stayed at the club and played a vital role in our promotion-winning season, not least the assist for Bobby Zamora's goal against Derby County in the Play-Off Final.

ADEL TAARABT

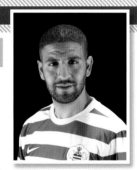

GIFTED attacker Adel Taarabt is fondly regarded by R's fans – not least for his contribution in our promotion-winning campaign of 2010/11 under Neil Warnock. His 19 goals and 19 assists helped fire QPR to the Championship title, earning the former Tottenham Hotspur man another crack at the top flight in the process. The Moroccan international didn't quite light up the Premier League in the same fashion the following season but did score vital goals towards the end of the campaign as Rangers avoided the drop. Following QPR's relegation in 2012/13, Taarabt was loaned to Premier League side Fulham, before joining Italian giants AC Milan for the second half of the season. A former trainee with Lens, Taarabt moved to Spurs and was twice loaned to Rangers before a permanent switch in 2010.

MIDFIELDERS

SHAUN WRIGHT-PHILLIPS

DIMINUTIVE winger Shaun Wright-Phillips joined QPR from Manchester City on deadline day of the 2011 summer transfer window, signing a four-your deal in the process. Capped 36 times by England, Wright-Phillips – the adopted son of former Arsenal favourite Ian Wright – began his career with City before a big-money switch to Chelsea in 2005. The midfielder returned to City just three years later but would be back in west London after moving to Loftus Road. Wright-Phillips has scored six goals for England and starred at the 2010 World Cup in South Africa but hasn't featured for the Three Lions since October that year. Wright-Phillips made 13 appearances for the R's last season.

STRIKERS

CHARLIE AUSTIN

WHAT a debut season for Charlie Austin at QPR! Having joined from fellow-Championship side Burnley in the summer of 2013, Austin netted 20 goals for the R's to steer the club to promotion success, including a brace in our 2-1 Play-Off semi-final win against Wigan at Loftus Road. Austin's start to professional football was a late one with his move to Swindon Town only coming at the age of 20. That followed after an impressive spell with Poole Town where he scored a staggering 48 goals in 43 games. That was enough for the Robins to hand him his first professional break, with Austin having previously worked as a bricklayer. He scored 37 goals in 65 matches before joining Burnley in 2011 where he hit another 45 goals in 90 outings prior to his move to Loftus Road.

BOBBY ZAMORA

BOBBY Zamora wrote himself into QPR folklore with one swing of the left boot, as he scored a sensational 90th minute winner in the Championship Play-Off Final against Derby County in May 2014. The talented frontman made an incredible impact in our Play-Off campaign, helping the club come from behind to beat Wigan in the semi-finals before THAT goal at Wembley Stadium in front of almost 90,000 fans. Zamora joined the R's from west London neighbours Fulham in January 2012 and almost instantly proved to be a key addition. His hard-working performances in attack helped Rangers to five home wins in a row at the end of the 2011/12 campaign – enough to see QPR avoid relegation. Zamora struggled with injuries in 2012/13 but had a never-to-be-forgotten campaign in 2013/14 to help fire the R's to promotion. Barking-born Zamora – who has two England caps – began his career with Bristol Rovers and has also played for the likes of Brighton & Hove Albion, Tottenham Hotspur and West Ham United. In July 2014 he signed a one-year extension, keeping him at Loftus Road until the summer of 2015.

SUMMER SIGNINGS

MAURICIO ISLA

VERSATILE Chilean Mauricio Isla was an ever-present for his country at 2014's summer World Cup showcase in Brazil. He made three appearances at right-back, and one on the right-hand side of midfield. He can also play in central and left midfield. That the 26-year-old is comfortable further forward will be important in the 3-5-2 formation Harry Redknapp is keen to deploy this season, with Isla a particularly adventurous full-back.

Developing through the youth system at Universidad Catolica in Chile, Isla started off as a striker, although soon realised his qualities were better suited to other positions. A sparkling performance in the Under-20 World Cup in 2007 for his country led to Udinese agreeing a deal with Catolica even before he had made a single appearance in the senior side. He

played at Udinese for five seasons, making 152 appearances in all competitions – scoring seven goals and providing 21 assists – before Juventus swooped to sign him at the beginning of the 2012/13 season for a fee in the region of £12.3 million.

However, despite featuring on 29 occasions in his first term with Juve, Isla struggled to keep a regular berth last season, yet still managed 18 Serie A outings and commanded a regular spot in Jorge Sampaoli's Chile side. With 51 caps for Chile and two international goals to his name, however, R's boss Harry Redknapp will be hoping Isla's experience for club and country proves key as the Hoops prepare for their return to the Barclays Premier League.

JORDON MUTCH

A FORMER England under-21 international with a blossoming reputation as one of the brightest young midfield prospects in the English domestic game, Jordon Mutch's arrival from recently-relegated Cardiff City is another positive addition to Harry Redknapp's QPR squad.

After starting out as a youngster with Derby County, for whom he featured at various age-group levels, Mutch joined Birmingham City in 2008. Understandably at such a young age, he was made to wait for first team football with the Blues, going on loan to Hereford United, where he made three appearances.

Another loan move materialised in January 2010, this time to Doncaster Rovers, where he scored two goals in 17 outings. Later that summer, Mutch was sent on loan to Watford, where he found the net five times in 23 matches during the 2010/2011 season, impressing with his ability to adapt to the rigours of the Championship. After returning to his

parent club Birmingham, he took his tally to two goals in 24 games by the summer of 2012, prior to putting pen to paper on a three-year contract with Cardiff City in a move rumoured to be worth in the region of £1.3 million.

It was during his two year spell with the Bluebirds that Mutch really developed as a player, playing a pivotal role in their promotion to the Premier League in 2012/13. He made 22 league appearances to help Malky Mackay's side to the title, and followed that up with a fantastic maiden season in the top-flight for the Welsh club. Seven goals and five assists in 35 appearances, of which nine were from the bench, made the Premier League stand up and take note of his talents, with his ability to play textbook box-to-box football at the highest level alerting a number of clubs. Fortunately for Redknapp and QPR, he chose a move to west London, signing a four-year deal at Loftus Road.

RIO FERDINAND

WITH a career the envy of most, Rio Ferdinand's move to QPR sees him reunited with the man who gave him his professional bow. R's boss Harry Redknapp brought Ferdinand on as a substitute for West Ham United in their final fixture of the 1995/96 season against Sheffield Wednesday. And the 35-year-old hasn't looked back since. Redknapp helped him develop into the world's most-expensive defender. He left to join Leeds United in an £18 million transfer five years later.

Ferdinand – who has 81 senior England caps to his name – has won just about all there is to in club football. He joins after 12 years at Manchester United – following a move from Leeds in July 2002 – and won six Premier League titles and the Champions League during his time at Old Trafford. Ferdinand has now retired from international football but won his first full England cap as a substitute for Gareth Southgate in a friendly against Cameroon at Wembley on November 15th, 1997.

At 19 years, eight days he became the Three Lions' youngest-ever defender. The Londoner was born in Peckham and trained with a number of clubs in the capital – including QPR – before joining West Ham's renowned youth system. Ferdinand has built a reputation as a composed central defender during a fine career to date. Redknapp, meanwhile, will no doubt hope his pedigree can help Rangers in our quest for Premier League stability.

STEVEN CAULKER

STEVEN Caulker's move to Loftus Road will see him reunited with former manager Harry Redknapp for a second time. A product of the Tottenham Hotspur Academy, centre-back Caulker made his professional debut in August 2009 whilst on a season long loan at Yeovil Town. Nearly ever present that campaign, he made 44 starts in League One as the Glovers finished a respectable 15th.

Caulker, 22, made his Tottenham Hotspur debut under Redknapp in September 2010 – a 4-1 League Cup defeat against Arsenal. Just five days after making his first Spurs appearance Caulker moved to Championship outfit Bristol City on loan until the end of the season. He made 29 appearances for the Robins and scored two goals, including one against QPR in a 2-2 draw in January 2011. However, his season was cut short when in March he sustained a knee injury ruling him out for the rest of the campaign.

After recovering from injury, Caulker joined newly promoted Premier League club Swansea City in June 2011 on a season long loan. He made four starts for the Welsh side before being ruled out for three months with a knee cartilage problem after colliding with the goalpost against Arsenal. He recovered in time to make 26 starts for the Swans who finished their debut season in the top flight in 11th spot. After representing the Great Britain side in five matches at the 2012 Olympic Games, the Feltham born defender signed a new four-year deal at White Hart Lane before going on to make 28 first team appearances in all competitions that season.

He scored his first Tottenham goal in a 2-0 win against Aston Villa with his performances being recognised with a call-up to the full England squad. Having previously represented the Under-21 side on 10 occasions, Caulker made his Three Lions debut in a 4-2 defeat against Sweden, scoring England's second goal.

Last summer however Caulker returned to Wales, this time on a permanent basis, to sign for newly promoted Premier League side Cardiff City in a deal worth £8m. The 6" 3' centre-back was ever present for Cardiff last term but he was unable to prevent them returning to the Championship at the first time of asking. Manager Harry Redknapp will be hoping Caulker can prevent a similar fate for QPR this time out as he joins Rio Ferdinand in a new look R's defence.

PLAYER PROFILES

SUMMER SIGNINGS

LEROY FER

Midfielder Leroy Fer, born in Zoetermeer, began his career with the Feyenoord youth academy at the age of nine. Advancing through the academy, he made his senior debut at the age of 17, impressing all and sundry with his well-timed box-to-box runs and excellent technical ability.

He made 103 league starts in total for Feyenoord, scoring 14 goals, winning two domestic honours in the process, before making a big-money move to FC Twente in 2011 for a reported £5.5million fee. Eight league goals in his first full season represented a fine return and he continued his impressive spell in his second term with the club, scoring five goals in 30 starts.

Norwich City was his next port of call at the start of the 2013/14 campaign, with the Canaries paying a fee believed to be in the region of £5million for the attacking midfielder's services.

Despite the Canaries eventual relegation from the top-flight, Fer was arguably their stand-out performer, making 32 appearances in all competitions for the Norfolk-based side, contributing four goals.

A call-up to the Dutch World Cup squad followed this summer, with his one and only appearance seeing him score with his first touch in the Brazilian showcase, heading home his sides opening goal in their 2-0 group stage win over Chile.

Rangers fans will be hoping the 24 year-old can make an equally spectacular start to life at Loftus Road.

EDUARDO VARGAS

Having begun his career at amateur level in Santiago, Eduardo Vargas joined Chilean top-flight side Cobreloa at the age of 17, and after a series of impressive performances, moved to Club Universidad de Chile – also in the top division – three years later. It was while with Los Azules that Vargas's profile grew, and it was only going to be matter of time before his talents took him away from his homeland.

In 2011, at the age of 21, he was short-listed for South American Footballer of the Year, eventually finishing runner-up to Brazilian forward Neymar. It was during the 2011 campaign that the talented forward hit 25 goals from 44 outings, a return which led Italian Serie A side Napoli to pay a reported £11.5m for his services.

Loan spells with Gremio in Brazil and Spanish outfit Valencia followed, and it was while at the Estadio Mestalla that Vargas scored two and created three goals from eight appearances to guide the club to the semi-finals of the 2013/14 UEFA Europa League.

On the international stage, Vargas made his debut in 2009 at the age of 19, and he played an integral part in his country's qualification for the 2014 World Cup, netting five goals to be his country's top scorer in the qualifiers.

Arguably Vargas's greatest individual moment to date came two months ago when he netted the only goal of the game as Chile beat Spain at the World Cup to reach the knockout stages, eliminating the Spaniards at the same time.

Now 24, QPR fans will be hoping Vargas can settle quickly into life in the Premier League.

CHARLIE WINS AWARDS QUADRUPLE!

CHARLIE AUSTIN CAPPED A REMARKABLE MAIDEN SEASON AT LOFTUS ROAD BY SCOOPING AN UNPRECEDENTED QUADRUPLE IN THE CLUB'S END OF SEASON AWARDS.

Austin – who scored 20 goals in all competitions for the R's – was voted Supporter's Player of the Year by the QPR fans, with over 33 percent of the vote.

The 25-year old was also named Ray Jones Player's Player of the Year by his team-mates, as well as winning the Kiyan Prince Goal of the Season award for his stunning strike against Charlton Athletic at Loftus Road in November.

Junior Hoops supporters also voted him as their Player of the Year, to complete a remarkable clean sweep for the former Burnley front-man.

Austin said: "To win all four awards is really special. I really didn't expect this in my first season, so I'm eternally grateful to everyone who voted."

Thanking the fans, he added: "I've managed to strike up a great relationship with the supporters and I'm ever so thankful to them for the awards.

"I just give everything I can every time I go over that white line – and every fan likes a goalscorer and luckily enough I'm one of them!"

FAN-TASTIC SUPPORT!

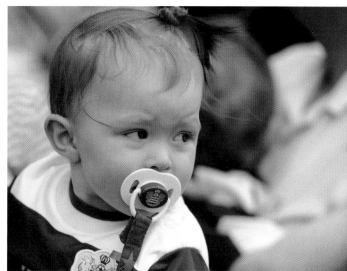

DRESSED TO IMPRESS IN THE PREMIER LEAGUE

PREMIER LEAGUE FOOTBALL IS BACK AT LOFTUS ROAD AND TO MARK THE OCCASION, THE R'S WILL BE WEARING THEIR FIRST EVER NIKE STRIPS FOLLOWING OUR RECENT ANNOUNCEMENT OF A FIVE-YEAR DEAL WITH THE WORLD'S LEADING SPORTS BRAND.

QPR trio Nedum Onuoha, Joey Barton and Charlie Austin unveiled the club's new home, away and third kits for the 2014/15 season at Nike's Phenomenal House in London in late May. The strips were revealed to an audience of Rangers fans, as well as R's boss Harry Redknapp, at a packed event in the capital.

The home kit features the classic royal blue and white-hooped design on the jersey, along with all-white shorts and socks. The away jersey boasts a bold red and black striped design, with a stylish V-neck collar. The away kit shorts and socks are both black, similar in style to a kit worn by the R's in the late sixties and early seventies.

The elegant and modern third kit comes in an all-white design, harping back to the kit worn in our famous League Cup triumph of 1967.

Nike Dri-FIT technology and engineered mesh material construction helps players stay dry and cool on the pitch, increasing breathability and air flow where athletes need it most, to help the team perform at the highest level. The five-year partnership will see Nike provide apparel, training kit and equipment for the R's until at least May 2019.

QPR QUIZ

Q1. Which R's defender plays at right back and wears the number 2 shirt?

Q2. Who received a red card in the 13/14 Championship Play-Off Final at Wembley?

Q3. Who scored the winning goal in the Play-Off Final at Wembley to clinch QPR promotion back to the Premier League?

Q4. Who scored the R's two injury-time goals against Middlesbrough to snatch a 3-1 away victory back in March?

Q5. From which London rivals did QPR sign Ravel Morrison on loan in January until the end of the season?

Q6. Who were Rangers' opponents in the first round of the League Cup which ended in a 2-0 victory for the R's, and who were the goal scorers?

Q7. Which QPR player got sent off in our 3-0 away defeat at Sheffield Wednesday?

Q8. In the 13/14 season which player started the most games for the R's?

Q9. Which QPR player won the Sky Bet Player of the Month in March?

ANSWERS ON PAGE 61

Q10. Throughout the 13/14 season how many goals did QPR score (not including cup games and Play-Offs)?

Q11. In the same 13/14 season how many goals did we concede (not including cup games and Play-Offs)?

Q12. Which R's captain has been with the club through both recent promotions to the Premier League?

Q13. Which Canadian midfielder had the most assists in the last campaign and with how many?

Q14. Which Spurs loanee wore the famous number 10 shirt during the promotion season just gone?

Q15. Which ex-England manager and QPR first team coach joined Derby County during the 13/14 season?

Q16. Which two players scored for QPR on the opening day of the season?

Q17. Which R's youngster notched a last-gasp winner on his QPR debut vs Ipswich Town?

Q18. Rangers' first defeat in the Championship came in late October away to which club?

Q19. How many clean sheets did Rob Green keep in the Championship fixtures including Play-Offs?

Q20. Which was the only first team fixture during the 13/14 season in which Julio Cesar played in goal?

PRE-SEASON DIARY

25.06.14 CLINT COMMITS

SO, after weeks of replaying THAT goal over and again so much that the play and rewind buttons on my handset have now all-but faded, the first snippet of news ahead of 2014/15. And how welcome it is too!

Club captain Clint Hill signs a one-year contract extension to keep him at QPR until the end of the new campaign.

No transfer news as yet but you get the feeling that plenty is bubbling under. Harry Redknapp has been a frequent visitor to Loftus Road in the last week or two for meetings with CEO Philip Beard and other senior club officials.

The press report that we have agreed a deal to sign former Manchester United and England defender Rio Ferdinand – incorrect at this time, although talks are ongoing, we are told by the CEO.

01.07.14 PLAYERS RELEASED

JUST over a month after promotion, the club announce details of player departures.

Out-of-contract men Stephane Mbia, Andy Johnson, Hogan Ephraim, Luke Young, Aaron Hughes, Angelo Balanta and Tom Hitchcock have all been released.

Meanwhile, preliminary discussions have taken place with Ale Faurlin, Rob Green, Gary O'Neil, Armand Traore and Bobby Zamora, whose contracts have also expired.

02.07.14 ALE RENEWAL

SEVEN days on from the first renewal – and another fans' favourite signs on for the year.

This time it's Faurlin, the popular Argentine who cruelly missed much of last season owing to a second cruciate ligament injury.

Ale tells QPR Player, the club's online TV channel: "I just want to play football." Fingers crossed he has a full season in the Premier League to show everyone just what he's all about next term.

04.07.14 ANOTHER DAY, ANOTHER EXTENSION

THE third contract renewal of the summer. Traore pens a new, two-year deal at Loftus Road to keep him at the club until mid-2016 at the very least.

Injuries aside, Traore did well last season in his newly-found position of left midfield and looks at home here now. Hopefully he can improve further still in 2014/15.

Off the pitch, there is also plenty else to keep the press team busy.

Works to improve our media facilities at Loftus Road are now well underway to bring us up to Premier League requirements.

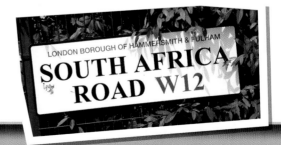

LONDON BOROUGH OF HAMMERSMITH & FULHAM
SOUTH AFRICA ROAD W12

A new press seating area is being built in Ellerslie Road, as is another TV studio in South Africa Road. The media room needs work plus there are three more TV interview positions to be installed near the tunnel ahead of August 16th, to add to the two we have already.

The camera pits at each end of the pitch have also been extended to allow for more operators.

10.07.14 PLAYERS RETURN

IT seems like only yesterday that we were leaving Wembley, Play-Off winners' trophy in hand, but here we go again.

Pre-season starts with two days of tests at the state-of-the-art Allianz Park, Hendon – home to Saracens Rugby Club – as the players are put through their paces.

The likes of Joey Barton, Charlie Austin, Danny Simpson and Nedum Onuoha all return, while Faurlin and Matty Phillips – both previously out with long-term injuries – also take part as they aim to be involved for the start of the new campaign.

10.07.14 GREEN SIGNS ON

CONFIRMATION that Green has agreed a new two-year contract with QPR. A fourth contract renewal of the summer at Loftus Road following deals for Hill, Faurlin and Traore.

The goalkeeper – voted man-of-the-match in the Play-Off final win over Derby County in May – told us: "I'm really pleased to have signed the contract. The first thing on my mind, after relaxing and enjoying winning promotion, was to get my future sorted.

"At the start of last season all I was focused on was playing football – thankfully that happened and we got promoted at the end of it all. This season is very much the same. I want to play week in, week out.

"We want to aim high, but we won't get carried away. We learnt a lot of lessons last time, so we will keep our targets in-house and be fully focused on the season ahead."

14.07.14 BACK AT HARLINGTON

A DOUBLE session awaited the players on day one of pre-season training.

That's set to be the case for the rest of the week, too. Head of fitness Carl Serrant has made it a tough first day back for the players in the searing heat – it's the hottest week of the year so far, in fact.

16.07.14 GOAL HERO ALSO COMMITS

SUMMER contract renewal number five, as Zamora becomes the latest player to sign up for the new season.

I interview Bobby for QPR Player and, of course, we start by talking about the goal at Wembley.

He admits that it all still hasn't quite sunk in yet. You're not the only one, Bobby – I still can't quite believe it happened when watching the highlights back! And I'm sure I'm not alone.

18.07.14 #RIOSIGNS, SAMBA MOVE

IT'S officially started! Centre-back Rio Ferdinand becomes new signing of the summer number one after penning a year's contract at Loftus Road.

We announce the deal on a sun-drenched Thursday evening after the 35-year-old popped into the stadium to put pen to paper.

Ferdinand tells us: "I used to sit in the Loft – my dad used to bring me here as a young boy. QPR was the first professional club to ever sign me.

"There are great memories for me here – for my family. Anton had nothing but good things to say about QPR and I watched Les here as a boy, with the likes of Ray Wilkins, Clive Wilson, David Bardsley and Alan McDonald.

"I spoke to Harry and Mr. Fernandes at length. I think they both looked me in the eye and knew that I still have something to offer – that I had a genuine desire to come here and play football. The draw for me was to play in the Premier League – and back here where it all started.

"It's not about money – I had loads of more lucrative offers available to me. I still feel I've got something to offer and I'm excited about helping this club cement its place in the Premier League."

In other news, midfielder Samba Diakite has joined Saudi Arabian top-flight side Al Ittihad on a season-long loan deal. The Malian international, 25, joined Rangers permanently following a number of excellent performances while on loan from Nancy in 2011/12. However, having struggled to impress again since, Diakite will now spend the campaign away from Loftus Road after time on loan at Watford last season. He has made 23 appearances for the R's in all, scoring one goal.

21.07.14 GERMANY BOUND – #RSINGERMANY

FERDINAND now in tow, it's destination Germany as the players board a 4pm flight to Leipzig from London Luton for the first of two pre-season tours.

After a bumpy flight – and a couple of delays en route, we arrive at the Bio-Seehotel, Zeulenroda around 10.30pm in a separate car, with the players arriving half an hour later.

Dinner is served on arrival for the squad, who head up to their rooms straight after following their day on the move.

22.07.14 #STEVENSIGNS, ROT-WEIß ERFURT 0, QPR 1

DAY two of our Germany tour has proven to be a busy one!

It would end with a victory on our first pre-season outing. Unsurprisingly, a 22nd-minute Austin header was the difference, following Barton's assist.

Earlier, the squad partook in their first two training sessions of the tour, with time put in on the training field both in the morning and afternoon.

Shortly before kick-off against Rot-Weiß Erfurt, summer signing number two.

Twitter was a hive of activity as chairman Tony Fernandes first broke news of the capture of Cardiff City defender Steven Caulker. Fernandes excited – so too boss Redknapp, who told us: "Steven's a top player, so we're delighted to have him at QPR.

"I know the ability he has and I think it's an important signing for the club – for the here and now, and for the future. I had him at Tottenham and I was very surprised when they decided to let him go last summer, because I thought he had a big future there.

"He's young; he's a good age; he's already a fine player but he has so much more potential – it's a really excellent signing for the club."

23.07.14 #RSINGERMANY: DAY THREE
A MORE relaxed start to the day following last night's victory.

Breakfast was consumed before the players enjoyed a session in a nearby swmming pool.

Then it was lunch, followed by training out on the pitch in the afternoon – around 4pm. The team were joined by Caulker, who arrived at our hotel two hours earlier.

We have been to the local Italian restaurant with Redknapp and the team this evening. There appears to be great camaraderie within the squad.

Barton and Simpson are currently the main culprits, the former constantly teasing the latter on his friendship with fellow former Manchester United man Ferdinand.

The pair have taken to our official media channels to taunt each other – something I'm sure you'll all see.

The highlight of the evening came in the form of the initiation sing-songs!

New boys Ferdinand, Caulker and a number of travelling youngsters took to the stage – much to the delight of the rest of the squad.

26.07.14 RED BULL LEIPZIG 2, QPR 0, GERMANY RETURN
TWO more days of double sessions followed before the R's rounded off their tour of Germany with a 2-0 reverse against second-tier outfit RB Leipzig.

Leipzig – like Erfurt – were playing their final pre-season match.

The home side are fancied for promotion this season and certainly backed up such support in a deserved win. Yussuf Poulsen was at the double for Leipzig.

The friendly saw both Ferdinand and Caulker make their R's debuts, while trialist Jack Collison was also given a run-out.

However, two second-half strikes from Poulsen were key, as Leipzig ran out victors at Stadion Der Freundschaft.

Following the fixture, we were off home – landing at Luton Airport at around 9.25pm.

28.07.14 GRANERO DEPARTS

SPANISH midfielder Esteban Granero has joined Real Sociedad.

The 27-year-old, who spent time on loan with the La Liga side last season, has penned a long-term contract after QPR accepted an undisclosed fee for his services.

Granero joined QPR in the summer of 2012, making 23 starts and five substitute appearances in the 2012/13 season, and scoring one goal.

He spent last term on loan with the Spanish side, making just four appearances owing largely to an anterior cruciate ligament Injury.

29.07.14 LEYTON ORIENT 2, QPR 2

AFTER introducing Ferdinand to the media for the first time as a QPR player at a specially-arranged press conference at Harlington, Rangers were back in match action at Brisbane Road in a 2-2 friendly draw against Leyton Orient.

Fielding a mixture of first-teamers and Under-21 players, Junior Hoilett and Barton were both on target.

Romain Vincelot's bullet header gave the hosts the lead early on. Hoilett soon levelled with an excellent effort, before Barton sent home a free-kick in the 47th minute.

But Dean Cox produced a tidy finish to restore parity in the 84th minute.

30.07.14 SOUTHEND UNITED 0, QPR 0

ANOTHER mixed side was named for the trip to Roots Hall – and another stalemate followed.

With Austin given a run-out at Leyton Orient – and Zamora out with a slight knock – Rangers were unable to field a recognised striker against Southend United.

Chances were few and far between in this contest versus League Two opposition.

If anything, the hosts enjoyed the better chances – Brian Murphy twice saving from Irish counterpart Barry Corr in the first period.

31.07.14 #RSINIRELAND

QPR have been on the move again – this time to Ireland for our second tour of the pre-season campaign.

The players and staff were back at Luton Airport for a 5pm flight to Dublin, landing around an hour and a half later.

Out of those who didn't travel to Germany, Adel Taarabt has flown out as he bids to step up his fitness, so too has Yun Suk-Young following a break after his World Cup venture with South Korea in Brazil.

Loic Remy is expected to arrive on Sunday after his move to Liverpool fell through.

02.08.14 SHAMROCK ROVERS 0, QPR 4

QPR ran out 4-0 winners against Shamrock Rovers, with Hoilett and Austin grabbing a brace each.

Hoilett opened the scoring on 13 minutes with a cool finish from inside the box before Austin doubled the advantage, heading home a Barton corner midway through the first half.

Hoilett made it 3-0 with a long-range effort on 89 minutes, and Austin wrapped up the scoring in injury time with another trademark header from eight yards.

05.08.14 #JORDON SIGNS, ATHLONE TOWN 0, QPR 2 – AND HOME AGAIN!

YESTERDAY, there was an open training session where hundreds of R's fans turned out to watch their team and take autographs.

Today? Another busy one in the QPR press office. Jordon Mutch, one of few shining lights in Cardiff's relegation season of 2013/14, moves to Loftus Road on a permanent deal – much to the delight of Redknapp.

"Jordon's a fine young player, with a big, big future," he said. "He's already shown what he can do at this level with Cardiff last season with a decent goals return – and this move will provide him with a great platform to take his game on to the next level.

"He wants to learn and improve his game. He's a good pro with a great attitude and this is a big opportunity for him at QPR."

Meanwhile, later in Athlone, another victory as the curtain comes down on our Ireland tour.

Goals either side of half-time from Zamora and Austin ensured Redknapp's side recorded two wins from two during their six-day long stay just outside Dublin.

Following the fixture, players and staff caught an 11.30pm flight home, landing back in England at 12.55am.

Just to add, O'Neil – who played a major part in our promotion campaign last term – joined Norwich City today. Good luck, Gary!

06.08.14 #MAURICIO SIGNS

MAURICIO Isla – who starred for his native Chile at the World Cup – joins on loan from Juventus.

The player was at Loftus Road yesterday to sign his deal and pose for photos, but we are only just able to confirm after waiting for all formalities of the deal to be finalised.

The 26-year-old told us: "I am very happy to be here – this is the start of an exciting, new adventure for me.

"Everybody knows that the Premier League is the greatest league in the world and the QPR proposal is very interesting, one I am very excited about.

"I hope this coming season is going to be great for both the club and myself. I will give 100 per cent in every game to help QPR in the Premier League."

09.08.14 ONE WEEK TO GO

AFTER another couple of days of training, Greek outfit PAOK are the visitors to Loftus Road today for the final fixture of our pre-season campaign.

With just one week to go until the start of the Barclays Premier League season against Hull City, another rollercoaster ride is almost upon us.

WORDSEARCH

FIND THE 18 WORDS IN THE GRID. WORDS CAN GO HORIZONTALLY,
VERTICALLY AND DIAGONALLY IN ALL DIRECTIONS.

K	D	B	N	B	B	V	Y	L	Z	G	X	D	K	Y	C
Y	K	W	I	F	W	K	H	N	O	T	R	A	B	T	T
D	T	G	T	N	C	T	S	P	L	H	I	L	L	T	T
O	P	P	S	T	K	U	B	F	R	T	T	N	N	E	E
Y	Q	W	U	D	K	R	N	K	T	U	H	M	K	L	L
L	N	Q	A	Y	P	O	A	B	V	D	M	A	N	I	I
E	N	E	O	X	S	K	P	N	P	K	R	N	H	O	O
R	C	U	E	I	L	D	V	M	J	O	G	E	N	H	H
T	N	N	R	R	E	R	Y	R	M	C	N	Y	O	H	H
G	R	R	D	N	G	R	Y	A	H	R	A	D	S	F	F
R	O	A	N	H	D	O	Z	Y	Y	R	G	R	P	L	L
M	G	U	O	Z	C	N	R	H	M	X	Y	P	M	Z	Z
N	D	N	B	R	S	E	H	G	U	H	L	X	I	M	M
Q	Y	N	Y	K	E	I	O	N	U	O	H	A	S	R	R
M	P	C	T	H	R	L	M	T	R	D	J	C	K	N	N

Austin	**Henry**	**Morrison**	**SukYoung**
Barton	**Hill**	**Murphy**	**Traore**
Doyle	**Hoilett**	**ONeil**	**Zamora**
Dunne	**Hughes**	**Onuoha**	
Green	**Kranjcar**	**Simpson**	

ANSWERS ON PAGE 61

47

2014/15 NIKE KITS
ARE OUT NOW

AVAILABLE FROM THE QPR SUPERSTORE
OR AT WWW.SHOP.QPR.CO.UK

The QPR goal-machine that is Charlie Austin was instrumental in the R's promotion winning campaign of 2013/14. The 'Superhoops' number 9 notched 20 goals last term, this despite a prolonged period on the sidelines due to a shoulder injury sustained at the end of January. Charlie Austin's two strikes against Wigan Athletic in a sensational and atmospheric Play-Off semi-final second leg at a rainy Loftus Road ensured that the boys from W12 made it through to Wembley for a showcase Play-Off Final showdown against Steve McClaren's Derby County. We all know what happened there! Relive Charlie's goals and celebrations in pictures as we pay tribute to...

"CHARLIE, CHARLI
CHARLIE, CHARLIE

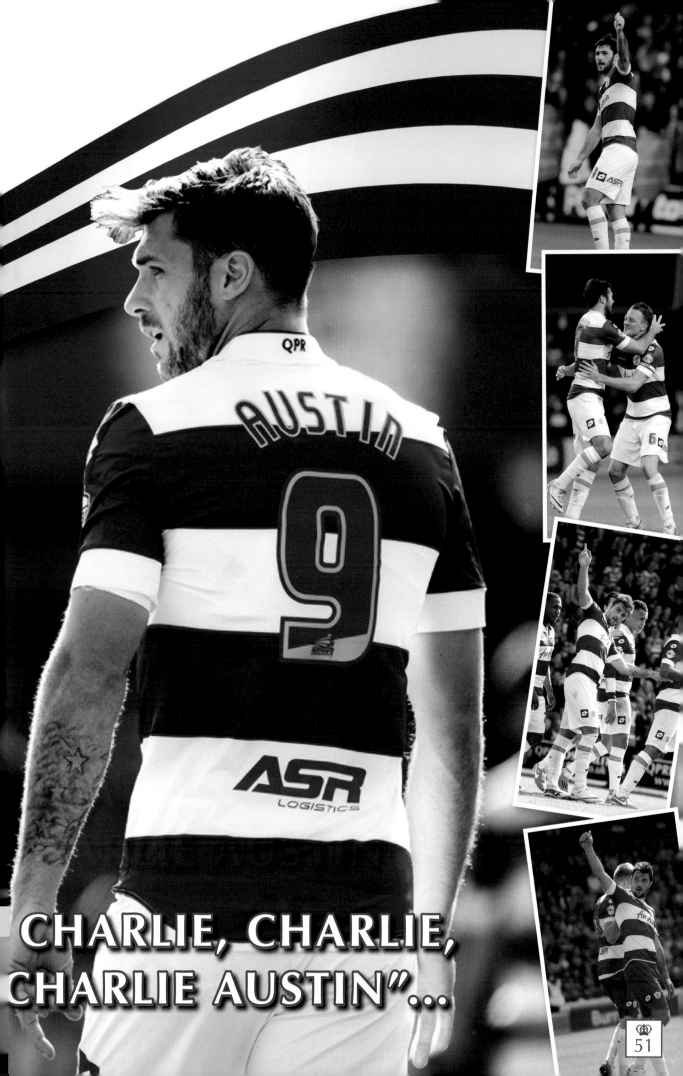

CHARLIE, CHARLIE, CHARLIE AUSTIN"...

RIO FERDINAND INTERVIEW

EXCLUSIVE INTERVIEW BY IAN TAYLOR

How big a role did Harry Redknapp play in you joining QPR?

Any player will tell you that if a manager gives you your first chance, your first steps in football, then there's a place imprinted in your heart really. That's not an opportunity that too many people get in their lives. He gave me that and he was forever supporting me when I got in the first-team. He always sung my praises. He told me off when I needed to be told off and put an arm around my shoulder when I needed it. He has that type of personality. We would go six months sometimes, maybe longer, without speaking, but when I saw him it was like back in the day. I've known Jamie and his other son Mark for years as well so it has always been that kind of connection. It's always been there.

Has he changed much since those days at West Ham?

Not really. He hasn't even got any grey hairs so I don't know what is going on. He is still the same really.

What is he expecting from you this season?

To play as many games as I can and as well as I can. To stay out on the pitch and on the training field. He mentioned about the amount of experience I have got and the years I have played the game – if I can be any help to the younger players coming through, in the way I train and conduct myself on the training pitch, then that's great.

the aim to play every game?

I was fit to play almost every game for Manchester United last season, but it's not to be all the time. I'm here and if the manager calls on me to play, which will hopefully be every week, then I am confident I will be able to produce.

Has retiring from international duty with England, coupled with your individual training programme, prolonged your career?

That's why I did it. If I didn't I would have been retired already. That's what happens when you stop playing international football. I didn't know I could recharge my batteries like I did when I stopped playing for England. It's great to feel as fresh as I do at this stage of my career.

How far off your very best do you feel?

I am a different player now as I am older, that goes without saying. Your powers are different. So you have to adapt and change your game a little bit. It is hard to gauge percentage-wise what the difference is. I might be playing quicker in my head than I was in my body back then.

Why QPR, when you could have retired and probably walked straight into a top TV role?

I was in Brazil with the BBC for the World Cup, sitting in my hotel room when it was raining, and I was thinking 'I can't wait to get back to training.' I was desperate to get back training and playing again. You meet problems head on. Even when I was at United and things were not going well, it makes you want to make you work harder. I think that will be the case here and there may be points in the season when we don't get the results that we want or expect, then you have to meet that head on, push harder and galvanise the troops and yourself.

What will be deemed a good season at QPR?

If we stay up here it will be an unbelievable achievement. That's why I'm here, because I feel there is still something to play for. If I had gone to a couple of the other clubs that were interested there wasn't really something for me to play for that I would have thought 'that's a great achievement for me'. This, staying in the Premier League with QPR, would be an amazing achievement.

Could part of your role this season be about changing the mentality around the squad to nurture them into winners?

Maybe yeah, but I've always been someone who leads by example through the way I play and train. Hopefully that can be a good and positive factor in the dressing room.

Would you have packed it in if QPR didn't come in for you?

Yeah, if I couldn't find a club in London I would have packed it in. Because of my family, we were desperate to come back to London.

Is coaching something you want to do in the future?

Yeah, I'm doing my badges at the moment. I'm at the B stage. I started years ago, just before I had my back problems. I had to stop because of that and I couldn't do it. I'd like to think I'll be a manager. That's how I feel now, but over the last four years I've wanted to be a manager, a coach, work with kids, and do TV! Whenever I end my career, we'll see how I feel then.

Loftus Road and Harlington are a bit different to what you're used to at Unite. What will you miss the most?

This is a bit more rustic, isn't it? I played here (at Harlington) as a kid, when Chelsea were here. We used to batter Chelsea every week. It's just different, you've got to adapt. At United, it's almost like you're in cotton wool – everything is done for you, laid out. Everything is done for you and laid out here too, but the soft furnishings probably aren't the same. But I'm not really bothered about that. I'm more interested in how we do on the pitch.

Loftus Road is renowned for its atmosphere, is that something you're looking forward to experiencing this season?

Yeah. I'm looking forward to that. It's a nice tight ground, old-school. I'm looking forward to playing in front of the QPR fans here. When I've been to Loftus Road with United, you know it's a hard place to come. Hopefully, we can recreate that this season.

INTERESTING FACTS

1895 – QPR entered the F.A cup for the first time, losing the 1st round to Old St.Stephens.

Before the start of the 1948/49 season, QPR became the first British team to make an official trip to play in Turkey. They lost one of four games to the Turkish Olympic side 2-1.

When QPR signed George Goddard he was working part-time at a local bus company.

Before his time at QPR, Tony Ingham served in the Royal Navy during the Second World War and also completed an electrical apprenticeship.

In 1997 Clive Allen appeared for American football team London Monarchs as kicker.

The first QPR game at Loftus road under floodlights was on 5th October 1953 vs. Arsenal. Arsenal won 3-1.

Before Les Ferdinand played for QPR he worked as a delivery driver, van steam cleaner and a plasterer's mate.

After retiring Dave Thomas became a P.E teacher at Bishop Luffa School in Chichester.

In 1963 Frank Sibley became the youngest player to play for the R's at the age of 15 years 275 days.

Gerry Francis was the only QPR player to have captained England whilst playing at the West London club. He captained the senior side 8 times.

QPR's record victory was at home to Tranmere rovers in December 1960 with the R's running out 9-2 winners.

Les Allen, his sons Clive and Bradley along with his nephew Martin have all played for the QPR first team. Martin's brother Paul is the only Allen in the footballing family not to appear for the west London club.

QPR were Southern League champions in 1911/12 and were invited to play in a charity shield match. The £262 proceeds were sent to the Titanic disaster appeal.

The 1908 FA Charity Shield was the first Charity Shield, a football match contested by the winners of the previous season's Football League and Southern League competitions. The match was played on 27 April 1908 between 1907–08 Football League winners Manchester United and 1907–08 Southern League champions Queens Park Rangers. The match was played at the neutral venue of Stamford Bridge, London, and ended as a 1–1 draw, goals coming from Billy Meredith for Manchester United and Frank Cannon for Queens Park Rangers.

In 1926 the club's original colours of green and white were changed to blue and white hoops.

In 1931 QPR relocated to White City Stadium which had a 60,000 capacity before returning to Loftus Road in 1933/34.

In 1980 Clive Allen was sold to Arsenal for £1.25 million. Before kicking a ball in a competitive match for his new club he was swapped for Crystal Palace's Kenny Sansom. Both players subsequently ended up in W12 over the following seasons. Allen came back to QPR in 1981 and Sansom signed for the R's in 1989.

Evelyn Lintott was the first QPR player to gain full England international honours. He received his first full cap in 1908 against Ireland.

QPR STATS

Highest League Loss:
1–8 – vs Manchester United 19 March 1969 Division 1

Oldest Player:
Ray Wilkins – 39 years 352 days. 01/09/1996 Division 1

Most Goals in Total Aggregate:
George Goddard, 186, 1926–34

Highest Attendance:
35,353 – vs Leeds United, 27 April 1974, Division 1

QUIZ ANSWERS

SPOT THE BALL PAGE 19

QPR QUIZ
PAGE 36

1. DANNY SIMPSON
2. GARY O'NEIL
3. BOBBY ZAMORA
4. BOBBY ZAMORA AND RAVEL MORRISON
5. WEST HAM UNITED
6. EXETER CITY, CHARLIE AUSTIN AND DANNY SIMPSON
7. RICHARD DUNNE
8. CLINT HILL
9. RAVEL MORRISON
10. 60
11. 44
12. CLINT HILL
13. JUNIOR HOILETT. 6
14. TOM CAROLL
15. STEVE MCCLAREN
16. NEDUM ONUOHA AND ANDY JOHNSON
17. TOM HITCHCOCK
18. BURNLEY
19. 20
20. EVERTON AWAY IN THE FA CUP

WORDSEARCH
PAGE 47

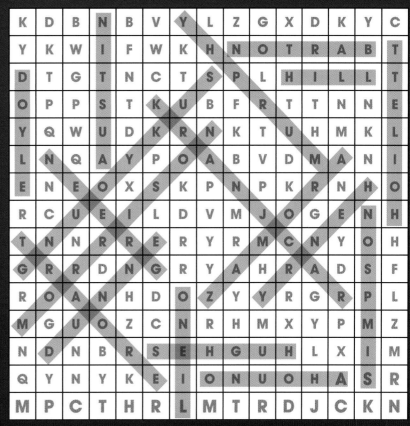